Dear Parents:

Congratulations! Your child is taking the first steps on an exciting journey. The destination? Independent reading!

STEP INTO READING® will help your child get there. The program offers five steps to reading success. Each step includes fun stories and colorful art or photographs. In addition to original fiction and books with favorite characters, there are Step into Reading Non-Fiction Readers, Phonics Readers and Boxed Sets, Sticker Readers, and Comic Readers—a complete literacy program with something to interest every child.

Learning to Read, Step by Step!

Ready to Read   Preschool–Kindergarten
• big type and easy words • rhyme and rhythm • picture clues
For children who know the alphabet and are eager to begin reading.

Reading with Help   Preschool–Grade 1
• basic vocabulary • short sentences • simple stories
For children who recognize familiar words and sound out new words with help.

Reading on Your Own   Grades 1–3
• engaging characters • easy-to-follow plots • popular topics
For children who are ready to read on their own.

Reading Paragraphs   Grades 2–3
• challenging vocabulary • short paragraphs • exciting stories
For newly independent readers who read simple sentences with confidence.

Ready for Chapters   Grades 2–4
• chapters • longer paragraphs • full-color art
For children who want to take the plunge into chapter books but still like colorful pictures.

STEP INTO READING® is designed to give every child a successful reading experience. The grade levels are only guides; children will progress through the steps at their own speed, developing confidence in their reading.

Remember, a lifetime love of reading starts with a single step!

Published in the United States by Random House Children's Books, a division of Penguin Random House LLC, 1745 Broadway, New York, NY 10019, and in Canada by Penguin Random House Canada Limited, Toronto.

Step into Reading, Random House, and the Random House colophon are registered trademarks of Penguin Random House LLC.

Visit us on the Web!
StepIntoReading.com
rhcbooks.com

Educators and librarians, for a variety of teaching tools, visit us at RHTeachersLibrarians.com

ISBN 978-0-593-43198-6 (trade) — ISBN 978-0-593-43199-3 (lib. bdg.)
ISBN 978-0-593-43200-6 (ebook)

Printed in the United States of America

10 9 8 7 6 5 4 3 2 1

DC LEAGUE OF SUPER-PETS

by David Lewman

illustrated by Sean Galloway
and Rosa la Barbera

Random House 🏠 New York

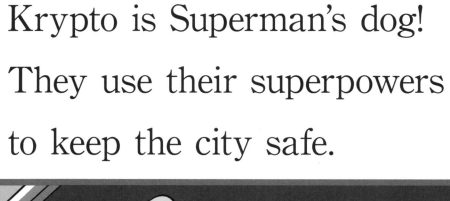

Krypto is Superman's dog!
They use their superpowers
to keep the city safe.

4

They are best friends.
Superman thinks Krypto
needs an animal friend, too.

At a nearby animal shelter, Krypto meets Chip, PB, Lulu, Merton, and Ace.

When a piece of Orange
Kryptonite gives Lulu
mind powers, she plans
to rule the world!
The other shelter
animals get powers, too.

PB can shrink and grow.

Ace becomes super-strong.

Chip shoots lightning.

Merton moves super-fast.

Lulu escapes and uses Green Kryptonite to take away Superman's and Krypto's powers.

Krypto asks the shelter pets
to help him save Superman.

They say yes!

Lulu gives other
guinea pigs superpowers
with the Orange Kryptonite!

Lulu and her army lock
the Justice League in cages.

Krypto and his friends try
to save the Justice League.

But Lulu puts them
in cages, too!

Lulu uses more Orange
Kryptonite to give herself
even more power!

The Green Kryptonite wears off and Krypto gets his powers back.

Krypto frees the hero pets!
Lulu's army attacks.

Krypto and his new friends don't back down!

They work together to
defeat Lulu and
her army.

Krypto frees Superman.

PB frees Wonder Woman.

Ace frees Batman.

Chip frees Green Lantern.

Merton frees The Flash!
The Super Heroes
adopt the Super-Pets!

Now Krypto has friends. Together, they are the League of Super-Pets!